ANIMAL ARK

The Lonely Pony

Lucy Daniels

With special thanks to Janet Bingham
For Katie. With thanks to Sarah and Pablo.
Illustrations by Jo Anne Davies for Artful Doodlers

ORCHARD BOOKS

First published in Great Britain in 2019 by The Watts Publishing Group

1 3 5 7 9 10 8 6 4 2

Text copyright © Working Partners, 2019
Illustrations copyright © Working Partners, 2019

A CIP catalogue record for this book
is available from the British Library.

ISBN 978 1 40835 412 4

Printed and bound in Great Britain by CPI Group (UK) Ltd, Croydon, CR0 4YY

The paper and board used in this book are made from wood from responsible sources.

Orchard Books
An imprint of
Hachette Children's Group
Part of The Watts Publishing Group Limited
Carmelite House
50 Victoria Embankment
London EC4Y 0DZ

An Hachette UK Company
www.hachette.co.uk
www.hachettechildrens.co.uk

CONTENTS

CHAPTER ONE

"Here it comes!" gasped Sam Baxter.

Amelia Haywood caught her breath.
A chestnut-coloured horse broke into
a canter a few metres in front of her.
The rider crouched low in the saddle as
the horse dashed towards a pyramid of
logs lying across the muddy ground. Its

muscles flexed under its gleaming coat. Then it sailed over the jump.

"Hooray!" cheered Amelia. She and Sam were sheltering in a marquee next to the muddy race course. It was Amelia's first ever cross-country event, and it was pouring with rain. But even so, excitement buzzed through the crowd.

The next horse and rider trotted on to the course. Sam glanced at his watch. "There are two-minute gaps between

each horse," he explained, raising his voice over the chattering crowd and the rain spattering on the marquee's plastic roof. "It's so they don't get traffic-jams at the jumps."

Amelia grinned. *At least someone knows the rules!* She had seen horse races on TV before, so she'd thought that all the horses would set off together. But in a cross-country race, there was no starting line. Instead, a timer was started when each horse took the first jump and stopped when they reached the end of the course. The horse that did it the fastest won!

The chestnut horse was galloping towards the next jump, made out of a picnic table. Amelia cheered again as the horse leapt over and galloped on into a copse of trees. Then a grey horse streaked up to the first jump, its rider leaning forward, cheeks flushed.

"I wish I knew how to ride!" Amelia said, sighing wistfully.

Sam nodded. "Me too! Hey, shall we see if Mr and Mrs Hope need any help?"

They pulled up the hoods of their raincoats and hurried to the next marquee, their wellies squelching in the mud. The marquee was filled with stalls, and the Hopes were sitting by a trestle table loaded with medical equipment.

"How's it going?" asked Amelia,

hurrying over to the two vets.

Mrs Hope smiled and raised a polystyrene cup of tea. "No emergencies, thank goodness!"

"We can all take it easy for now," said Mr Hope.

Amelia felt a rush of pride at the way Mr Hope said "we". She and Sam were official helpers at Animal Ark, the surgery run by the Hopes.

Sam nudged her. "Look at that tiny pony!"

Amelia turned round. A man

was leading a golden pony into the
marquee. It was small and sturdy, with a
long, shaggy mane. Its tail almost swept
the ground!

"Oh!" Amelia squealed in delight. "It's
so cute!"

The man led the pony to a stall with
a banner that read "Speedwell Pony
Homes".

Amelia and Sam glanced at each
other, grinned, and hurried over.

"Hello!" said the man, as he took off
his wet rain jacket. "I'm Joe. Have you
come to meet Ginger?"

Amelia nodded. "Please could we
stroke him?"

"Go right ahead," said Joe. "Ginger loves being petted!"

Ginger was almost the same height as Amelia. A forelock of mane fell over his face, and when Amelia brushed the fringe aside, big, gentle, long-lashed eyes stared back at her. The pony's wide nostrils flared as he nuzzled her jacket. Amelia felt her heart melt.

"What kind of pony is he?" asked Sam, patting Ginger's thick mane.

"He's a Shetland," explained Joe. "He

used to be a companion to a racehorse. He and the horse were special friends, and Ginger helped keep him calm before races. But now his owner's moved abroad, so we're trying to find him a new home."

He handed Amelia and Sam a leaflet each. "*Speedwell Pony Rehoming*," Amelia read out loud. "*Matching Ponies with Forever Homes*." Underneath was a photo of Ginger and a phone number.

"Poor Ginger," Sam said.

"Can we help give out the leaflets?" asked Amelia.

Joe beamed. "That's very kind of you! Here, take a pile of them."

As more children gathered to meet

Ginger, Amelia and Sam went back to the course, the leaflets in their jacket pockets. The rain had almost stopped, but the ground was slippery under Amelia's wellies.

They walked past the log jump and along the edge of the field, towards a copse of trees. As they passed a jump made of planks of wood fixed between two tree trunks, they heard approaching hoofbeats.

Turning, Amelia saw a big, brown horse with a white stripe on his face thundering down the track, with a young woman on his back. They were getting closer and closer to the jump.

Too close! thought Amelia. Her heart lurched with alarm. *They're going to run straight through it!*

At the last moment the horse threw up his head and jumped. His front legs cleared the plank, but his left back hoof clattered against the fence. *CLUNK!*

The horse landed on the other side and stumbled.

"Oh no!" cried Sam.

The rider slid from his back as the horse jerked his head and tottered on three legs. She hung on to the horse's reins, her face creased with worry under her black riding helmet. "Whoa, Walnut!" she said.

"The horse is limping," said Sam. "He needs help!"

"We're going to get the vets!" Amelia called over to the rider.

"Please hurry!" she called back.

Amelia's heart pounded as they sprinted to the marquee – and not just from the effort. She was worried about the horse and the tent seemed a very long way away. *We've got to get there fast,* thought Amelia as she ran, *before that horse hurts itself any more!*

CHAPTER TWO

A few minutes later, Amelia and Sam hurried back on to the race course with the Hopes. The young woman had managed to coax her horse to the edge of the course, out of the way of the horses still galloping past.

"Thanks for coming so quickly," the

rider said. "I'm Fran, by the way. This is
Walnut."

Mr and Mrs Hope introduced
themselves, then Amelia and Sam.
"They're a big help at our surgery,"
said Mr Hope, and Amelia couldn't help
beaming with pride.

Mr Hope held Walnut's reins

while Mrs Hope unzipped a bag of equipment.

"He shied at the jump," Fran explained. "He knocked his left hind leg, but I'm not sure if he's hurt or just worked up. He gets like this sometimes …"

"Let's take a look," said Mrs Hope.

"Try to hold him still."

"Stay well back," Mr Hope warned Amelia and Sam. "Horses can kick, so you must never stand behind one."

Mr Hope and Fran held Walnut's head between them, and he seemed to calm a little. Amelia hadn't realised just how big the horse was – more than twice the size of little Ginger. He had a rich brown coat, and his tail and mane were almost black. His neck muscles tensed as he swung his powerful head from side to side. His chest heaved, and his coat was soaking even though the rain had stopped. When he tossed his head, flecks of foam flew off his muzzle.

Mrs Hope took off the protective pads that were fastened around Walnut's lower legs, then ran her hands down his left hind leg. "Could you pass me the hoof-pick, Amelia? It's the curved metal hook."

Amelia found the hoof-pick in the bag and passed it to Mrs Hope. The vet lifted Walnut's leg and tapped the underside of the hoof. Walnut swished his tail and Fran murmured soothing words.

"He looks really sweaty," said Sam. "Maybe he's got the flu or something?"

Mr Hope shook his head. "The sweating is normal after a big workout," he explained. "Galloping around is really hard work!"

"And Walnut worked up a sweat even before the race began," added Fran. "He was kicking inside his horsebox all the way here."

Mrs Hope pressed the end of a stethoscope to Walnut's chest. Amelia knew she was listening to his lungs and heart.

Fran looked sad and Amelia felt a

throb of sympathy. "Where did you learn to ride, Fran?" she asked, hoping to cheer her up.

"At Welford Stables," said Fran. "In fact, I'm a riding instructor there now."

"That's really cool!" said Sam.

Amelia glanced at him and knew they were both thinking the same thing. *Maybe we can learn how to ride there, too!*

"All's fine with Walnut," said Mrs Hope, taking off the stethoscope. "I advise rest and hosing his leg with cold water, just as a precaution." She zipped up her medical bag. "But he's clearly very agitated," she said gently. "It might be safer not to race him for a while."

Fran nodded, but her eyes filled with tears. "You're right," she said. "I've had to pull him out of a few races now." She rubbed her eyes and patted Walnut's muzzle. "I wish I could help him relax."

Amelia looked on helplessly. She wished she could help too! *But how … ?*

The next Saturday morning, Amelia was walking through Welford Village to the Old Mill Bed & Breakfast, owned by Sam's parents. She felt like she might burst with excitement. *We're going riding today!*

Her mum and Mr and Mrs Baxter

had agreed that she and
Sam could have lessons
with Fran, so Amelia
was wearing her new
riding gear – leggings, a
smart jacket, and boots
with a low heel. Fran
had promised that the
riding school would
lend her a helmet.

Amelia had also brought her stack
of leaflets about Ginger. *Everyone at the
stables loves horses and ponies*, she thought.
Maybe someone there can give him a home.

The front door of the B&B was open.
Amelia walked into the large hallway

to see Sam slumped in the chair behind the reception desk. His Westie puppy, Mac, trotted over to Amelia, his tail wagging.

"Hi, Mac," said Amelia, patting his curly white fur. "What's up, Sam?

Don't you want to go riding?"

"Look at me!" wailed Sam, coming out from behind the desk. He was wearing a tweed jacket two sizes too big for him. The pattern was a red and hot-pink check.

On his legs he wore orange jodhpurs
and his yellow wellies.

"Oh," said Amelia, trying to keep a
straight face. "You look very … bright."

Sam picked up a purple helmet from
the desk and plonked it on his head.
Amelia couldn't hold it in any more,
and let out a giggle.

"Whoa!" she laughed. "Where did you
get that?"

"It's my cousin Meg's," said Sam
gloomily. "She's grown out of it,
but it fits me." He took it off again.
"Unfortunately."

"You know what?" said Amelia.
"Who cares what you're wearing? The

important thing is – we're going riding!"

Sam grinned. "It's going to be great, isn't it? Dad says he'll take us to the stables when he's finished serving the breakfasts."

Sam's mum, Mrs Baxter, came in through the lounge door, wearing a smart yellow dress. With her was a young woman with blonde hair pulled

up in an untidy bun.

"Let me get you your room key, Dr Rutland," said Sam's mum, walking over to the reception desk. "Oh, hello, Amelia!"

"Hi, Mrs Baxter," said Amelia.

"My son, Sam, and his best friend," Mrs Baxter explained to the guest. She took a key out of a drawer. "I hope you enjoy your stay. What brings you to Welford?"

"An arachnology conference," said Dr Rutland. "I'm looking forward to exploring the village."

Amelia wondered what arachnology was, but Sam's mum was already wheeling Dr Rutland's suitcase towards the stairs.

"Can I carry the rest of your luggage?" Sam offered politely. He went over to a big box wrapped up in layers of thick towel. But Dr Rutland rushed in front of Sam and picked it up herself. "No, thank you! Much better that I take this. It's, er … it's rather fragile." She followed Sam's mum up the stairs.

"That was weird," said Sam. "Why didn't she want me to help?"

"Maybe your jacket put her off?" teased Amelia.

"Oi!" said Sam, but he grinned.

Mr Baxter came through into the hallway, pulling on his coat. "Who's ready to go riding?"

"Me!" said Amelia and Sam together.

CHAPTER THREE

Welford Stables had a concrete courtyard, surrounded on three sides by a low, whitewashed building. The dark-green stable doors had their top halves open, and horses looked out of many of them. In the nearest stable, stretching up to rest his chin on the door, was Ginger!

"Hello, Ginger!" cried Amelia. She went over to stroke the pony's shaggy mane. "I didn't expect to see you here!"

"Looks like you already know our tiniest resident!" Amelia turned to see Fran coming across the courtyard, wearing a fluorescent yellow instructor's bib.

"We met him at the cross-country

race," said Sam. "But what's he doing here?"

"The Speedwell charity is paying for him to stay until they find him a new home," Fran explained.

Amelia held up her stack of leaflets. "That's brilliant! We've brought these to help."

"Great!" said Fran. "I'll make sure all our students get one."

Ginger nuzzled Amelia's sleeve, and Fran smiled. "Would you like to help me take him out to the paddock?"

"Yes!" said Amelia and Sam. Fran unbolted the stable door and clipped a rope to Ginger's head collar. She handed the end of the rope to Amelia. "Just walk forward," she told her. "He knows what to do."

Amelia took a few steps across the courtyard, and Ginger clopped out of his stable behind her. Fran showed them the way out of the stable yard and on to the muddy track that led to the paddock. "This is amazing," said Amelia. "It's like waking Mac!"

She gave the rope to Sam so he could have a turn. "No, this is easier than walking Mac!" said Sam with a laugh.

They went through the gate and into the paddock – a grassy field with a fence down the middle. Fran unclipped Ginger's lead rope, and the pony trotted out into the field. On the other side of the fence, a horse was tossing his head and cantering up and down.

"It's Walnut!" said Amelia. "Is his leg OK?"

"Yes, it's fine," said Fran.

"He still seems really wound up," Sam pointed out.

Walnut snorted and bucked, staring at Ginger. The little Shetland pony snorted back, but didn't move away. Walnut neighed and reared up, kicking his hooves into the air. Ginger just gave

another snort and swished his tail.

"At least Ginger doesn't seem bothered," Fran said. Her eyes were sad. "All the other horses avoid Walnut now. I don't know what to do with him!"

"How did he get like this?" wondered Amelia.

Fran sighed. "He used to be bullied by the other horses in his old home," she said. "When we adopted him, I spent ages trying to socialise him. It was going well, until we started entering competitions. There are just too many other horses around at races! I'm worried I'll have to stop riding him altogether." She glanced at her watch.

"Time to start your lesson, guys. We'd better hurry."

Fran strode back to the stables, Sam following. Amelia hung back for a few moments to watch the horse and pony. Walnut neighed loudly, rearing up again. Ginger watched calmly. Walnut bucked twice, grunting. Ginger dipped his head to tear off some more grass. Then Walnut paused, staring at Ginger.

He must be confused! Amelia thought. *Especially if the other horses are all scared of him.*

But the little Shetland wasn't frightened of Walnut. He just carried on munching the grass. Finally, Walnut dipped his head and began grazing too.

Amelia grinned. "Wow!" she murmured. "Well done, Ginger – you've calmed him down!" She remembered what Joe had said about Ginger being a companion pony. "I bet you're missing your old racehorse friend," she said sadly. "Well, now you've got Walnut instead!"

She had to run to catch up with Sam and Fran. In the stable yard, Fran was greeting the other children in the class, and kitting everyone out with a helmet and riding gloves. Amelia felt a flutter of excitement – her first ever riding lesson was about to begin!

"The first thing to remember,"
Fran began, "is always make sure a
pony knows you are there before you
approach it …"

As Fran spoke, another class rode into
the stable yard. They followed their
instructor past Amelia's group, and
Amelia spotted Tiffany Banks from her

year at school,
riding a white
pony. Tiffany
noticed Amelia
and Sam and
scowled.

*She doesn't
look happy to see*

us! thought Amelia. She waved anyway.

Instead of waving back, Tiffany nudged the girl riding beside her and pointed at Sam. "Check out that purple helmet! He looks like he's wearing a giant grape. And as for that jacket …" She and her friend sniggered.

Sam's jaw clenched.

"Then again," Tiffany went on, loud enough for Sam and Amelia to hear, "he doesn't even know how to get on a horse, so no wonder he doesn't look like a real rider."

Amelia glared at Tiffany. "Ignore her," she whispered to Sam as Tiffany and her class moved on. "She's always going on about how she's such a good rider. She's probably just annoyed we're here."

Some older kids led the ponies out of their stalls. "Meet your ponies and your leaders," said Fran. "They're experienced riders, and they'll help you with everything."

There weren't enough leaders to pair with all the students, so Fran helped Amelia. Her pony was light brown with patches of white. He was bigger than Ginger, but a lot smaller than Walnut.

"This is Pippin," Fran said, rubbing the pony's ears. "He'll take good care of you. Stand on the mounting-block, Amelia. Take the reins loosely in your left hand and hold them on the pommel." Fran patted the bump at the front of the saddle. "Now put your foot in the stirrup and swing your other leg over …"

Amelia settled into the saddle and held the reins. She could hardly believe it. *I'm actually sitting on a pony!*

Fran led Pippin around the yard with the other ponies. The rocking motion felt strange at first, but Amelia couldn't stop grinning. She looked across at Sam, who was riding a brown pony with three white socks, led by a teenage boy with red hair. Sam's eyes were shining.

"Wow!" he said, when Amelia's pony drew up to his. "This is so cool!"

Fran led Amelia and Pippin out of the yard, and the other ponies followed. They clopped along the muddy lane and into a fenced area with a sandy surface like a playground.

"This is the sand school," said Fran. "The ground is made of sand and rubber pellets, so don't worry if you fall off – it's soft."

They all laughed, though some of the laughter sounded a bit nervous. Amelia felt a bit nervous too, but mostly excited.

As the leaders guided the ponies around the soft surface, Amelia looked around. From Pippin's back she could see the old farmhouse where her friend Caleb Parish lived in the distance. She could even see Llarry and Lliam, his pet llamas. Amelia and Sam had convinced the Parishes to adopt them, as well as some chickens and pigs.

Hang on a minute …

Amelia gasped as an idea struck her. *That's how we can help Ginger,* she thought. *The Parishes can adopt him!*

CHAPTER FOUR

The next day, Amelia rang the doorbell of the Parishes' farmhouse.

"By the way," said Sam, who was standing next to her on the doorstep, "I looked up 'arachnology'. You know, what Dr Rutland does. It's the study of spiders. Isn't that weird?"

Amelia laughed. "It's probably pretty interesting. I watched a TV programme about spiders the other week. There's one type from the Amazon rainforest that measures thirty centimetres across."

Sam's eyes widened. "No way!"

"It's called the bird-eating spider," said Amelia. "But they're not dangerous to people."

Sam shuddered. "I still wouldn't want to find one in the bath! I'm not great with spiders. It's the one thing I don't like about living in the countryside – all the creepy-crawlies!"

The door opened. "Hi, guys!" said Caleb, greeting his friends. "Do you want to come and see the animals?"

Chickens strutted along beside them as they walked over to Llarry and Lliam's field. Caleb gave Amelia and Sam chunks of apple to feed the llamas. They held them out in the palms of their hands, and the llamas bent their long necks down to eat them. Amelia chuckled as Llarry took a piece with his soft lips.

When the llamas had finished eating
the apples, Caleb led Amelia and Sam
across the farmyard.

"Whoa!" cried Sam. "I didn't know
you had goats!"

The goat pen was a wooden hut on
stilts, attached to ramps and platforms
at different heights. Three small goats

scrambled down to see them, prancing
with excitement.

Caleb opened the gate into the
pen. "Meet Milly, Tilly and Dilly. We
adopted them from Mr Stevens's farm.
Izzy's mum helped us build the pen."

One of the goat kids gently butted
Amelia's leg. She stroked the kid's hard
little head and scratched her coarse,
white coat. "She's adorable," Amelia
said. "You've got so many animals now,
Caleb."

Her friend grinned. "That's not all!"

He showed them into a barn with
chicken-wire runs attached along two
outside walls. Inside were pens holding

guinea pigs nibbling straw and rabbits lolloping about.

"Cool!" said Sam.

Amelia picked up a guinea pig with black, brown and white patches. He sat calmly in her hands, chomping on a leaf. Amelia touched his floppy, petal-like ears, and laughed when he twitched his nose at her.

"What do you think of our new arrivals?" asked Mr Parish, as Caleb's parents strolled into the barn.

"They're brilliant!" said Sam.

"We've decided to try your idea, Amelia," said Mrs Parish.

Amelia's eyes widened. "You're going to start a petting farm?"

Caleb grinned. "It's opening next Saturday!"

"We're going to donate all the profits to local animal charities," said Mr Parish. "Perhaps you could ask Mr and Mrs Hope for some suggestions."

"Definitely," said Amelia. "This is amazing!" Then she suddenly remembered why they'd come. She pulled one of the pony rehoming leaflets out of her pocket and passed it to Mrs Parish. "Could Ginger be part of your petting farm?" she asked. "He really needs a home."

"We've met him a couple of times," added Sam, "and he's really gentle. I bet he'd love living here."

Caleb peered over his mum's elbow to read the leaflet. "Oh, please can we adopt him? We could give pony rides!"

But Mr and Mrs Parish both shook their heads.

"I'm sorry," said Mrs Parish. "I wish we could! But we don't have room for a pony now that we've got so many other animals."

Sam and Caleb groaned. Disappointment twisted at Amelia's heart, but she did her best to smile. "That's OK," she said. "I understand."

Amelia and Sam helped Caleb feed the rabbits and guinea pigs, then they walked back to the B&B.

When Sam opened the front door, Mac ran to greet them. He jumped up on his hind legs, yapping excitedly.

"It's nice to see you too, Mac!" said Sam, patting him.

Mac barked again and ran around in a circle, chasing his tail – and knocked into the sturdy legs of Mr Ferguson, who was wearing his

motorbike leathers and had his helmet tucked under his arm. He was a regular guest at the B&B and reminded Amelia of a grizzly bear.

Mr Ferguson tutted. "That wretched mutt! He trips me up every time."

"Sorry, Mr Ferguson," said Sam. "He just gets over-excited sometimes. Come on, Mac – I have to get my riding stuff."

Amelia and Sam climbed the stairs, with Mac hot on their heels. "I'll just be a sec," said Sam, popping into his room.

As Amelia waited, she noticed another bedroom door standing open.

"That's Dr Rutland's room," said Sam, returning with his jacket and helmet under his arm. "She must have forgotten to shut it!"

But as Sam went to close the door, Mac shot into the room. "No!" cried Sam. "You're not allowed in there!"

Amelia darted into the room, just in time to see Mac leap up at the bedside table.

CRASH! Something large fell to the floor, shattering in an explosion of glass. Soil showered on to the carpet and little shards of glass skittered everywhere.

"Mac!" gasped Amelia. The puppy stood in the middle of the floor, tail down and shivering. *Oh no!* she thought. *If he moves, he might step on broken glass!*

"I've got him!" cried Sam. He dumped his riding gear on the floor and swept Mac up in his arms.

Amelia checked the underside of the puppy's paws. "He's not injured," she said with relief. "But what did he break?"

They both stared at the glass shards.

"A fish tank?" guessed Sam.

"There's no water," Amelia pointed out. "It does look like a tank, though…" She felt the blood drain from her cheeks.

"Sam … Dr Rutland's job …"

Sam's jaw gaped open. "It's a spider tank!" He darted out of the room with Mac in his arms, then peered nervously around the doorframe. "Where is it? It had better not be one of those bird-eating ones! Oh, Mac, you've really gone and done it now …"

"Leave this to me," said Amelia. She picked up Sam's riding things and handed them to him. Then she searched the room, taking care to avoid the broken glass. She looked everywhere – in the bathroom, under the bed and behind the television table. There was no sign of a spider anywhere.

"I don't like this," said Sam, his eyes wide with fear.

Amelia shook her head. "Don't worry. I bet the tank was empty anyway," she said. She wanted to make Sam feel better, but she wasn't sure she believed it. *More likely*, she thought, *there's a spider on the loose …*

CHAPTER FIVE

"I'm glad you told me," said Mr Baxter, when Amelia and Sam explained about the broken tank. "Naughty Mac! I'd better go and clear up the broken glass."

While he went upstairs, Sam's mum drove Amelia and Sam to Welford Stables for their second riding lesson.

Their class was gathering in the stable yard, while the students from the advanced group were dismounting after their lesson. Tiffany slid down from her pony and frowned when she saw Amelia and Sam.

"Good, everyone's here," said Fran, ticking off the students' names on a clipboard. Then she paused, pen in the air, as a banging sound came from inside one of the stables.

"What's that?" asked Amelia.

BANG! The stable door rattled on its hinges.

"It's Walnut," said Fran, her face creased with worry. "Listen, guys. I need

to get him out
before he hurts
himself. Stay
well back and
keep quiet!"

Everyone
moved into
the middle of
the courtyard. Fran carefully opened
the stable door and slipped inside.
Amelia could hear her speaking slowly
and calmly inside the stall. Then the
instructor led Walnut out. The big horse
spun around, hooves raised high, and
snorted as he tossed his head. Fran
managed to loop the rope attached to

his bridle around a hitching post.

"I think there must be something wrong with him," said Fran, anxiously. "Wait here while I call Animal Ark. Nobody go near him!"

Fran hurried off into the main building. Walnut flicked his tail and dropped his head.

"Poor Walnut," said Sam. "He really doesn't look happy."

Tiffany shrugged. "I think he looks fine." She started to walk around Walnut, inspecting him.

"Be careful!" warned Amelia. "Mr and Mrs Hope said you mustn't go behind a horse, in case they kick!"

Tiffany stopped and went red. "Just because you do chores at Animal Ark doesn't mean you know anything about horses," she snapped.

"She was just trying to help," said Sam.

"I don't need any help!" said Tiffany. "I've been riding for ages. Way longer than you two."

Amelia's stomach lurched with worry. "But Fran said to keep away from him!"

"He obviously just wanted to be let out of his stable," said Tiffany, flicking her glossy ponytail. "I bet I could ride Walnut right now. Even without a saddle."

Everybody stared at her. Some of the other kids even looked impressed.

"Tiffany, you can't be serious," gasped Amelia. "It's far too dangerous!"

"For you beginners, maybe," said Tiffany. "But I'm an experienced rider. He doesn't scare me!" She untied Walnut's rope.

Amelia couldn't believe what was happening. Before she could stop her, Tiffany hopped up on to a mounting-block, grabbed Walnut's head collar and swung her leg over his bare back. Walnut stamped his hooves and snorted.

"You're not even wearing a helmet!" burst out Sam. "Here!" He hurried over and held up his own purple helmet.

Tiffany curled her lip, but she took the helmet. Then she froze. Creeping out from inside the helmet came a hairy leg. Then another. And another …

Tiffany shrieked. She dropped the helmet. It hit the ground, and a very large spider scuttled out.

"Spider!" screamed one of Tiffany's friends. Then the other kids began yelling and jostling each other to get away. Walnut reared up, punching the air with his front hooves. Watching in horror, Amelia saw Tiffany go flying. Then – *SPLAT!* – she landed in a heap of horse manure.

Walnut gave a furious neigh. With a toss of his head, he galloped across the courtyard, through the open gate and out into the lane. He jumped over the hedge and disappeared into a nearby clump of trees.

Amelia and Sam ran over to Tiffany. She was covered in horse poop and straw, and her face was clenched with fury. She tried to get up, but slipped in the manure. Sam reached out a hand to help her, but Tiffany angrily pushed it away.

"This is your fault," she snarled. "Why did you bring that … that *thing* here?"

At least she doesn't seem hurt, thought Amelia.

Sam was staring at the spider with wide eyes. He licked his lips. "I think I should tell Fran that Walnut's escaped," he said. Then he set off running towards the main building.

The spider was keeping very still on the concrete ground. Its body was round and its eight legs had orange and black stripes. *A tarantula*, Amelia guessed, remembering the spider programme she'd watched.

The other kids were panicking and jumping on to mounting-blocks to avoid the spider. *I've got to catch it so it doesn't get away!* thought Amelia.

Looking around desperately, she spotted a plastic bucket full of carrots for the horses. She tipped the carrots out on to the ground, snatched up a pair of riding gloves and pulled them on.

Amelia took a deep breath. She had never seen such a big spider before. Her hands were trembling.

"Come on, Amelia," she muttered to herself. "It's just like any other animal in trouble. I need to catch it before it gets hurt – that's what Mr and Mrs Hope would do."

The tarantula slowly lifted one fuzzy, orange and black leg and probed the air.

Her heart hammering, Amelia moved towards it, as quietly as she could. She crouched down beside the spider and reached for it …

CHAPTER SIX

Holding her breath, Amelia scooped
up the tarantula in her gloved hands.
She couldn't believe how light it was.
Carefully, she placed the spider inside
the bucket and quickly closed the lid. A
wave of relief washed over her.

"Whoa!" The other kids burst out

clapping and cheering. "That was amazing, Amelia!"

Sam and Fran came running into the courtyard, followed by two other instructors. One of them was speaking on a phone.

"Where's the spider?" cried Fran.

"Amelia rescued it!" someone answered.

"It's in this bucket," said Amelia.

Sam looked pale, but he grinned at her. "Nice one! I'm glad I didn't have to touch it."

"Well done for acting so quickly," said Fran. Then she whipped round to Tiffany. "Are you hurt?"

Tiffany pulled hay out of her ponytail. "No, but it was their fault for—"

"You've been very lucky, Tiffany," Fran snapped. "You know you're not allowed to mount any horse without an instructor present. And I said to stay away from Walnut! What were you thinking?"

Tiffany's lower lip wobbled.

One of the instructors had saddled up a gleaming black horse, and Fran swung up on to it. "I'm going to look for

Walnut. I hope he hasn't hurt himself!"
She galloped out of the stable yard.

The other instructor was still speaking
on the phone. "Thanks for your help,
Mr Hope," he said, scratching his beard.
"I'll call again when we've got Walnut
back."

"Can I speak to Mr Hope, please?"

asked Amelia. "About the spider."

The instructor passed her his phone, and Amelia explained quickly. "I've got it in a plastic bucket, but I don't know if it's hurt."

Mr Hope said, "Well done, Amelia. I'll come right away."

Amelia passed the phone back and Sam gave her a high-five. "I wish I'd seen you catch it!"

Amelia felt her face flush. "It was nothing really."

"I can't believe the spider was in my helmet!" said Sam, with a shudder. "Can you imagine if I'd put it on?"

Amelia grinned. "It probably thought

your helmet would make a nice new home!"

An hour later, Amelia and Sam were in the assessment room at Animal Ark. The tarantula was in a shallow tray, and Mr and Mrs Hope were examining it under a heat lamp. Sam kept hiding his face in his hands, but Amelia could see him

peeking through his fingers.

"It's important to keep tarantulas warm," Mr Hope explained. "They're from hot climates and they aren't able to warm themselves up. This one will have cooled down a lot during its adventure."

"It's been an adventure for us too," muttered Sam. "And not the fun kind!"

"The important thing is that it isn't hurt," said Mrs Hope. "A fall like that could have torn its abdomen or broken off a leg, but nothing's damaged. It's lucky you rescued it in time. Has anyone been in touch with the owner?"

Sam nodded. "I called Mum on

the way here. She said she'd tell Dr
Rutland."

Amelia leaned in to get a closer look
at the spider. The orange and black
segments of its legs were fringed with
long hairs. It sat very still, every now
and then gently feeling the air with the
tip of one leg. She saw Sam making a
face, and couldn't help giggling.

Dr Rutland
rushed into the
room, wide-
eyed. She gave
a sigh of relief
when she saw
the tarantula

on the table. "Octavia! Thank goodness you're all right!"

Mr Hope smiled. "Thanks to Amelia and Sam."

Amelia felt her face go red again. "Actually, it was all our fault …"

"My puppy Mac broke the tank," confessed Sam. "I'm really sorry he got into your room."

Dr Rutland waved a hand. "Please don't worry. Accidents happen, and I shouldn't have left the door open. I was in a rush to collect some specimens – Welford's full of wonderful spiders. I'm just grateful to you both for rescuing Octavia! I'd hate to lose her."

"The spider's a girl?" said Amelia.

"That's right," said Dr Rutland. "Female tarantulas live for a lot longer than the males. I've had Octavia for fifteen years."

Amelia blinked. "Fifteen years?"

"Yes, and she could live another fifteen." Dr Rutland smiled. "Tarantulas are a long-term pet!"

"You're brave to stay in the same room as her," said Sam, admiringly. "I wouldn't sleep a wink!"

"Whatever do you mean?" said Dr Rutland, laughing. She picked up the spider and cradled her in her hands. "Octavia is the cutest arachnid in the

whole world!"
Her eyes twinkled.
"Probably only
an arachnologist
would think that,
though. You know,
I'm giving a talk
on spiders next

Saturday. Would you two like to come?"

"Yes, please!" said Amelia.

"Er, I might be busy …" said Sam,
eyeing Octavia nervously.

"It's at the Parish Petting Farm's
grand opening," Dr Rutland said. "Do
you know it?"

Amelia and Sam gasped.

Mrs Hope chuckled. "They certainly do. I think most of the animals are there because of these guys!"

After Dr Rutland and Octavia had left Animal Ark, Amelia and Sam headed outside and began to walk to Amelia's house for lunch. Just as they were about to turn into her road, they heard the clip-clop of horses' hooves. A pair of riding instructors came trotting along the road.

"Hi, you two," said one of them. It was the man who'd phoned Animal Ark. "Have you seen Walnut?"

Amelia's heart sank. "Oh no! Is he still missing?" In all the excitement of rescuing Octavia, she'd almost forgotten about the runaway horse.

"I'm afraid so. Fran couldn't find him anywhere, so we're all out searching now. He could be miles away already!"

A cold shiver raced down Amelia's spine. *Poor Walnut!*

"We'll help look for him," she said. "Won't we, Sam?"

Sam nodded. "You bet!"

CHAPTER SEVEN

A short while later, Amelia and Sam
were searching the woodland close
to Welford Stables. Sam had fetched
Mac, and the little Westie puppy was
scampering excitedly around their feet.

"Go, Mac!" Sam said. "Find Walnut!"

A startled rabbit bolted out from

under some bracken and Mac set off after it. The rabbit vanished among the trees, and Mac trotted back to Sam with his tongue lolling.

Amelia chuckled. "He's good at chasing rabbits, but I think he needs more practice with runaway horses." She sighed. "Where could Walnut have got to?"

Suddenly, Mac's ears pricked up. He barked again and hurtled off between the trees.

"Come back!" called Sam. "You've chased enough rabbits today, Mac!"

They hurried after him, following flashes of his white fur between the tree trunks. The puppy ran into a sun-filled clearing, then doubled back and raced up to Sam, jumping up at his knees.

"What is it, Mac?" asked Sam.

The dappled light on the far side of the glade was full of shifting shadows. A movement caught Amelia's eye – something swishing back and forth, like a branch – or a tail …

Her heart leapt. "It's Walnut!" she cried.

They ran across the glade. The big horse was standing beneath a beech tree. His eyes were circled with white, and his ears were flattened towards the back of his head. Suddenly he reared up,

crashing his front hooves back down to the ground and shaking his mane.

Amelia and Sam stepped back, but at the same time Mac darted forward, yapping at the horse.

"Mac!" yelled Sam. "Come here!"

Walnut backed away, eyes swivelling madly. He stomped the ground, tail swishing, as Mac barked.

"He'll be trampled!" gasped Amelia. "Do you have any treats?"

Sam fumbled in a pocket and brought out some doggy choc drops.

"Mac!" Sam and Amelia called together.

At last the little Westie scampered back, and Sam clipped on his lead as Mac guzzled down the choc drops. "Phew," said Sam. "Mac was getting Walnut even more upset!"

"All animals seem to," said Amelia, sadly.

Then something struck her. *Not* all *animals* … She clicked her fingers. "I've got it!"

Sam looked puzzled. "Got what?"

"No time to explain," said Amelia. "You and Mac stay here and keep an eye on Walnut. I'm going to run to the Parishes' house – it's not far."

She dashed off through the woods. Her legs were aching by the time she burst out of the trees, and a stitch was pulling at her sides. Caleb and his parents were feeding the goats behind their house. "Hey!" Amelia called, hurrying over to them. "We need help!"

"What's wrong?" asked Caleb.

Amelia explained in a rush. "Please can I call the stables?"

"Of course." Mrs Parish found the

number on her
mobile. She handed
Amelia the phone
just as Fran picked
it up.

"Fran!" cried
Amelia. "It's Amelia.
Sam and I found
Walnut!"

"Oh, thank goodness!" Fran said.

"Sam's with him now. He's in the
woods, in the clearing just north of the
Parishes' house."

"I'm on my way!" said Fran.

"Wait!" said Amelia. "Please can you
bring Ginger too?"

"Ginger?" said Fran. "But why?"

"I think he can help Walnut." Amelia hung up. Then she hurried back to the clearing with Caleb and his parents.

They found Sam sitting on a log holding Mac on his lap. To Amelia's relief, Walnut was still there.

"Walnut's still pretty cross," Sam whispered.

The big horse stamped his hooves and snorted.

"I hope Fran gets here soon," said Amelia.

They didn't have to wait long. Soon Amelia heard hoofbeats and looked up to see Fran trotting through the trees on

a spotty grey horse. She was holding a
lead rope attached to Ginger's bridle.
Walnut whinnied as they approached.

"It's all right, Walnut," Fran said. "We
want to help." She slid off the grey's
back and tied the reins to a branch.
"What's your plan, Amelia?"

They all turned to
look at her.

Amelia took
a deep breath.
"When Walnut
was wound up
before, Ginger
calmed him
down," she

explained. "Maybe he can do the same now."

Fran looked doubtful. "Are you sure?"

"It was after you'd left the paddock," Amelia explained. "Walnut was upset, but Ginger was so relaxed that he calmed down too."

"Sounds like it's worth a shot," said Mr Parish.

"Go on, Fran," said Sam. He pointed at Ginger, whose ears were swivelled towards Walnut. "See, he wants to help."

At last Fran nodded. "Let's give it try, then."

Amelia held her breath as Fran led Ginger towards Walnut. The big horse was stamping and snorting and tossing his head. Ginger trotted ahead of Fran, but halted in front of Walnut. He gave a little whinny.

Go, Ginger! thought Amelia.

Walnut leaned down and touched his nose to Ginger's. The pony nickered and Walnut snorted back.

They nuzzled each other, Walnut's brown face rubbing Ginger's golden one.

Now that Walnut was calm, Fran reached

out slowly and took hold of his bridle. Amelia wanted to cheer, but she was afraid of spooking Walnut again. Instead, she hugged Sam and Caleb. *It worked*, she thought. *It really worked!*

Grinning, Fran led Walnut and Ginger over to them. The two horses, one big and one small, were walking calmly, side by side. "That was a great idea,

Amelia!" said Fran. "They really do have a special bond." She sighed. "It's just a shame we can't afford to keep Ginger at the stables with Walnut for ever."

They walked back through the woods, with Fran leading Walnut and Mrs Parish leading the grey. Amelia and Sam took turns leading Ginger,

while Caleb held Mac's lead. Mr Parish walked alongside his wife, and Amelia could hear them talking in low voices.

At last Mr Parish cleared his throat. "Maybe Ginger and Walnut can stay together after all," he said.

Everyone looked at him in surprise.

"How do you mean?" asked Fran.

"Well," said Mr Parish, "we're planning to donate the profits from our petting farm to an animal charity – and we thought Ginger could be our charity."

"We'll use the money to pay for Ginger to stay at Welford Stables," said Mrs Parish. "He can live with Walnut, but he can come and visit the petting farm sometimes too."

Amelia's heart soared. "That's a brilliant idea!"

"What do you think, Fran?" Sam asked. "Please say yes!"

Fran beamed. "It sounds perfect!"

Amelia wrapped her arms around Ginger's soft neck and buried her face in his hair. "You've got a new home, Ginger!" she told him. "And a new friend."

CHAPTER EIGHT

It was the opening day of the Parishes' new petting farm. A chattering crowd of children filled the big barn, sitting on hay bales arranged around a trestle table. Amelia and Sam perched on one near the front.

On the table was a large glass tank.

Inside it was Octavia, her orange and black body gleaming like velvet.

The whole barn went quiet as Dr Rutland opened the tank and lifted the tarantula out. A couple of smaller children shrank back in fear.

"Meet Octavia, everyone," said Dr Rutland, smiling. "Don't worry – she won't hurt you."

Some children let out sighs of relief.

"Octavia is a Mexican redknee tarantula," Dr Rutland explained. "Like all pets, tarantulas need to be looked after carefully. Their tank must be kept warm and humid, and they need somewhere to hide."

The children sitting on the hay bales murmured excitedly.

"Now, who would like to hold Octavia?" Dr Rutland asked. "You'll need to wear gloves, so her hairs don't irritate your skin."

At first nobody raised their hand, and Dr Rutland looked disappointed. Then Amelia spoke up. "I'll hold her."

Dr Rutland beamed. Amelia took some thin rubber gloves from a pile on the table. Once she'd put them on, Dr Rutland gently placed the spider in her cupped hands.

It was different to when Amelia had picked Octavia up at the stables – this time she wasn't scared at all. She could only just feel where the tarantula's eight feet rested on her palms. The spider was so light, Amelia worried she might accidentally hurt her.

"Can I have a go?" Sam asked, pulling on some gloves.

"Are you sure?" asked Amelia.

Sam looked nervous, but determined. "I've been thinking. Octavia is kind of cute … you know, in her own way."

Amelia smiled and passed Octavia over to her friend. Sam stiffened as he held the spider. But after a few

moments his shoulders relaxed, and he began to smile too. "I can't believe I'm holding a tarantula! This is actually pretty cool."

"Who else would like a turn?" said Dr Rutland. This time several hands flew into the air. Dr Rutland took Octavia back and gently passed her around.

At the end of the talk, everyone clapped – very quietly, so Octavia wouldn't be scared. "Tarantulas don't have ears," Dr Rutland explained, "but they can sense noise with the hairs on their legs."

"Thank you, Dr Rutland," said Mr Parish, making his way to the front of the crowd. "That was fascinating." He paused. "And if you're looking for more spiders to study, there are plenty of them in our old farmhouse!"

Everybody laughed.

"Well," Mr Parish went on, "you've just met the smallest creature we have at the petting farm today. Now it's time to meet one of the biggest. Everyone follow me, please!"

Amelia, Sam and the other children filed out into the farmyard, where a miniature fairground roundabout with tiny cars was playing jingly music.

In the middle of the yard stood Fran and Ginger. The pony had blue and pink ribbons in his mane and tail and there was a garland of flowers around his neck.

There were gasps of delight among

the crowd. "So cute!" cried a little girl.
Ginger lifted his nose and whickered.
He seemed to be smiling at everyone as
children crowded round to pet his soft,
golden coat.

Fran caught Amelia and Sam's eyes
and waved. They grinned and waved
back.

"Can we ride him?" one girl asked.

"Ginger would love that," said Fran. "Who wants to go first?"

"Me!" cried several children at once, quickly lining up as Fran put a saddle on Ginger's back.

Caleb, Amelia and Sam brought out the guinea pigs to introduce to people while they waited their turn. Fran chatted to them as she helped a small boy up into the saddle.

"Walnut's completely recovered from his escape," she said happily. "And he's starting to relax, now that Ginger has moved to the stall next to him! I took them out in the horsebox the other day, and Walnut didn't make a bit of fuss. I can't wait to race him again!"

Amelia smiled. "That's wonderful news!"

The very last ride of the day went to Amelia. She climbed into the saddle, hooking her feet into the stirrups that hung on each side of Ginger's stocky body. She took the reins in her hands, just as Fran had taught her at the stables.

"Very good," said Fran. She led them around the farm with a rope hooked on to Ginger's bridle. As they rounded the farmhouse, she said, "Why don't you have a go by yourself?" Then Fran unclipped the lead rope and stepped back.

Amelia shivered with excitement. She lifted the reins as she'd been taught and Ginger clip-clopped on. Amelia twitched the reins and Ginger obediently turned left.

I'm riding, Amelia thought. Happiness fizzed through her like bubbly

lemonade. *I'm really riding, all by myself!*

When Amelia and Ginger arrived back

in the farmyard, she was grinning with triumph. Fran helped her dismount, and Amelia gave Ginger's shaggy, hay-scented neck a hug. "Thank you, Ginger. That was so much fun!"

The farmyard was full of people cuddling rabbits and guinea pigs. Llarry and Lliam, wearing brightly embroidered blankets, stood with Mr Parish at the centre of an admiring crowd. Mrs Parish was by the pig pen, answering questions about Daisy and Pip. Chickens were strutting about between everybody's feet, pecking up ice cream cone crumbs. The goats, on colourful leads, were running around

Caleb's legs like maypole dancers.

"How was your ride?" asked Sam, as Amelia went over to join him by the hen house.

"Great!" she said.

"Hey," said a familiar voice from behind them. Amelia turned to see Tiffany standing there. She was holding a black riding helmet under one arm.

"Hi, Tiffany," said Amelia, cheerfully. "What do you think of the petting farm?"

Tiffany nodded. "I guess it's OK." She chewed her lip, then suddenly thrust the helmet out at Sam. "This is my old one," she said. "You can borrow it if you

want. Instead
of the purple
one."

Sam looked
surprised, but
he beamed
and took the helmet. "Thanks, Tiffany!"

Tiffany shrugged. "You were right
about Walnut. I shouldn't have tried
to mount him – I was showing off.
Maybe I'll see you at the stables next
Saturday?"

"We'll be there," said Amelia.

"Wow," said Sam, as Tiffany headed
off to see the llamas. "I think I need an
ice cream after that! Want one?"

Amelia grinned and nodded.

"You know," said Sam, as they headed over to the ice cream van, "I have a feeling this petting farm is going to be a big success!"

"Of course it will," said Amelia. "Everybody here loves animals, just as much as we do."

Sam raised an eyebrow. "Are you sure about that?"

Amelia chuckled. "Well – *almost* as much!"

The End

Turn over for a sneak peek at
Amelia and Sam's next adventure!

Amelia looked up as a tall, strong-looking man entered, carrying a German Shepherd in his arms. He had short grey hair and a worried look on his face. Amelia saw that a patch of fur on his dog's foreleg was matted with blood. *Oh no*, she thought, hurrying to close the door behind him. *This can't be good …*

Mr Hope, the vet, crossed the reception, smiling kindly. "Hello," he said to the man. "I don't believe we've met before. What's happened here?"

The man nodded a greeting. "I'm Kent Jacobs. I've only just moved to Welford." The man stroked the dog's

head gently. "And this is Sherlock …
He went to explore some bushes near
our new cottage and came out with
this wounded leg. I've no idea how it
happened."

Mr Hope turned to Amelia and Sam.
"Do you two want to help me in the
consulting room?"

Amelia and Sam nodded. "Yes,
please!"

Julia, the receptionist, steered her
wheelchair around the reception desk.
"I'll keep an eye on Mac," she told Sam,
with a wink. "He can help me hand out
the treats – that's if he doesn't scoff them
all first!"

"Thanks, Julia," said Sam, as he and Amelia followed Mr Hope.

In the consulting room, they watched as Mr Hope and Mr Jacobs gently laid the German Shepherd on the examination table. Sherlock had a mixture of brown and black fur, a long, black nose and pointy ears. Amelia knew that German Shepherds were particularly calm and intelligent dogs, even though they looked really fierce!

Sure enough, Sherlock was patient and lay still as Mr Hope used a long tweezer to move some of the bloodied fur away so he could get a better look at the wound. A trickle of blood dripped on to the examining table.

Amelia leaned forwards so she could see better. *I've got to learn as much as possible if I'm going to become a vet one day,* she thought as she watched.

Read **Scaredy-Dog** to find out what happens next ...

Animal Advice

Do you love animals as much as Amelia and Sam? Here are some tips on how to look after them from veterinary surgeon Sarah McGurk.

Caring for your pet

1. Animals need clean water at all times.
2. They need to be fed too – ask your vet what kind of food is best, and how much the animal needs.
3. Some animals, such as dogs, need exercise every day.
4. Animals also need lots of love. You should always be very gentle with your pets and be careful not to do anything that might hurt them.

When to go to the vet

Sometimes animals get ill. Like you, they will mostly get better on their own. But if your pet has hurt itself or seems very unwell, then a trip to the vet might be needed. Some pets also need to be vaccinated, to prevent them from getting dangerous diseases. Your vet can tell you what your pet needs.

Helping wildlife

1 Always ask an adult before you go near any animals you don't know.

2 If you find an animal or bird which is injured or can't move, it is best not to touch it.

3 If you are worried, you can phone an animal charity such as the RSPCA (SSPCA in Scotland) for help.